The Story of NOAH

Illustrated by Pascale Lafond

A long time ago, there lived a man named Noah. Noah had lived a very long time. He was more than 500 years old! He was a very good man. This is the story of the most amazing thing that happened to him in all of his years.

During the time of Noah's life, God was upset with the people of the earth. He wanted them to live in love, but they were living in sin. So God decided He would flood the earth.

He chose one good man to help Him start again. That man was Noah.

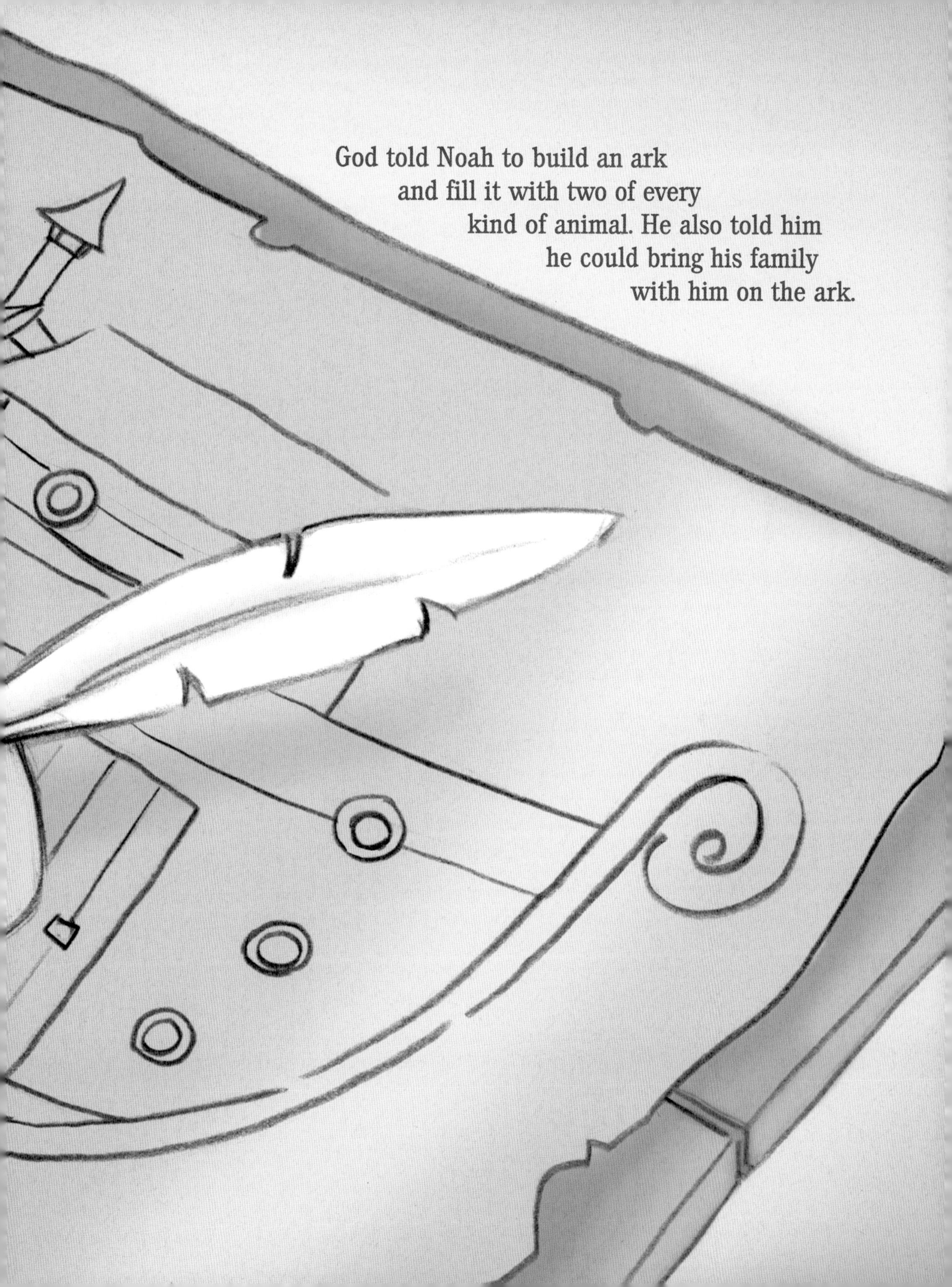

God told Noah to build an ark and fill it with two of every kind of animal. He also told him he could bring his family with him on the ark.

God gave Noah instructions for how to build the ark. He told him what kind of wood to use. He told him to make it three floors tall. He even told him to build a big door in the side. Noah built the ark exactly as God had told him to build it. The ark was HUGE!

The animals came two by two and filled the ark just as God had instructed. There were lions and tigers and bears and elephants and birds and giraffes and every other kind of animal you can think of. They all went on the ark so they would be safe.

Noah also brought his family with him on the ark. God told Noah to bring his wife, his three sons, and their wives. They all joined the animals on the ark.

Noah loaded the ark with enough food for his family and for the animals to last for many days.

There was nothing left to do but wait...

And then it started to rain...

It rained and rained and rained. For forty days and forty nights it rained. Noah's ark rose higher and higher as the rain came down. Noah and his family and all the animals were safe as the earth was flooded by this storm.

It rained so long, and so hard, that the rain eventually covered everything. Even the mountains of the earth were covered with rain. Nothing survived that enormous rain except for the people and the animals that had boarded the ark. They were grateful that God had chosen them.

Finally, the rain stopped. Noah and his family were pleased, but they still needed to stay on the ark because there was no dry land to walk on.

God sent a wind to help dry the earth. After many months, the land began to dry. Noah and his family needed to find the dry land, so Noah sent out a dove from the ark to try to find it. Eventually, the dove returned with a fresh olive branch, which was a sign that there was dry land ahead.

When they reached land, Noah and his family and all the animals left the ark behind. They now had to go out into the world and start again.

Noah thanked God for taking care of him and his family and all the animals. When they left the ark to go out and fill the earth, God promised never to flood the earth again.

As a sign of His promise,
God created a rainbow in the clouds.